Your Kind of Mommy

Marjorie Blain Parker

ILLUSTRATIONS BY **Cyd Moore**

· DUTTON CHILDREN'S BOOKS ·

Published by the Penguin Group · Penguin Group (USA) Inc., 345 Hudson Street, New York, New York 10014, U.S.A. · Penguin Group (Canada),
90 Eglinton Avenue East, Suite 700, Toronto, Ontario, Canada M4P 2Y3 (a division of Pearson Penguin Canada Inc.) · Penguin Books Ltd,
80 Strand, London WC2R ORL, England · Penguin Ireland, 25 St Stephen's Green, Dublin 2, Ireland (a division of Penguin Books Ltd) · Penguin
Group (Australia), 250 Camberwell Road, Camberwell, Victoria 3124, Australia (a division of Pearson Australia Group Pty Ltd) · Penguin Books
India Pvt Ltd, 11 Community Centre, Panchsheel Park, New Delhi - 110 017, India · Penguin Group (NZ), Cnr Airborne and Rosedale Roads, Albany,
Auckland 1310, New Zealand (a division of Pearson New Zealand Ltd) · Penguin Books (South Africa) (Pty) Ltd, 24 Sturdee Avenue, Rosebank,
Johannesburg 2196, South Africa · Penguin Books Ltd, Registered Offices: 80 Strand, London WC2R ORL, England

CIP Data is available.

Dutton Children's Books,
a division of Penguin Young Readers Group
345 Hudson Street, New York, New York 10014
www.penguin.com/youngreaders

Designed by Irene Vandervoort

Manufactured in China   First Edition
ISBN 978-0-525-46989-6

10 9 8 7 6 5 4 3 2 1

For Steve, Casey, and Rachel—my kind of kids—M.B.P.

For Lindsay and Branden—C.M.

If I could be an octopus,
I'd wrap eight arms around you....

But I'm not THAT kind of mommy,
and I know my hugs will do.

If I could be a shaggy dog,
my tail would wag for you. . . .

But I'm not THAT kind of mommy,
and I know my smiles will do.

If I could be a buzzy bee,
I'd make sweet honey for you. . . .

But I'm not THAT kind of mommy,
and I know my treats will do.

If I could be a wallaby,
my pouch would snuggle you. . . .

But I'm not THAT kind of mommy,
and I know my lap will do.

If I could be a humpback whale, we'd dive deep seas of blue....

But I'm not THAT kind of mommy,
and I know my love will do.

If I could be an elephant,
my trunk would sprinkle you....

But I'm not THAT kind of mommy,
and I know my baths will do.

If I could be a timber wolf,

I'd howl moon songs for you....

But I'm not THAT kind of mommy, and my lullabies will do.

And that's the best thing I could be!